# NICKELODEON

降 去 神 迹

# AVATAR
## THE LAST AIRBENDER

# THE LOST SCROLLS: AIR

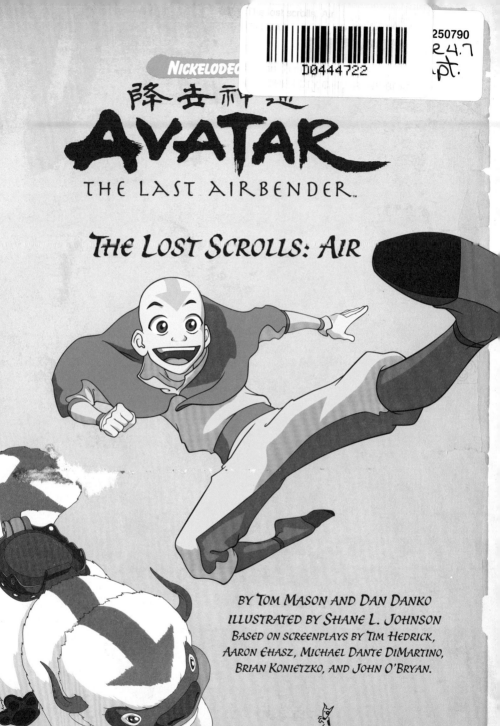

BY TOM MASON AND DAN DANKO
ILLUSTRATED BY SHANE L. JOHNSON
BASED ON SCREENPLAYS BY TIM HEDRICK,
AARON EHASZ, MICHAEL DANTE DIMARTINO,
BRIAN KONIETZKO, AND JOHN O'BRYAN.

SIMON SPOTLIGHT/NICKELODEON
NEW YORK    LONDON    TORONTO    SYDNEY

Based on the TV series *Nickelodeon Avatar: The Last Airbender*™as seen on Nickelodeon®

SIMON SPOTLIGHT
An imprint of Simon & Schuster Children's Publishing Division
1230 Avenue of the Americas, New York, New York 10020
© 2007 Viacom International Inc. All rights reserved. NICKELODEON,
*Nickelodeon Avatar: The Last Airbender*, and all related titles, logos,
and characters are trademarks of Viacom International Inc.
All rights reserved, including the right of reproduction in whole or in part in any form.
SIMON SPOTLIGHT and colophon are registered trademarks of Simon & Schuster, Inc.
Manufactured in the United States of America
10 9 8 7 6 5 4 3
ISBN-13: 978-1-4169-1879-0
ISBN-10: 1-4169-1879-5
Library of Congress Catalog Card Number 2006932879

# Prologue

降击神通

## IF YOU ARE READING THIS,

you have uncovered one of the four hidden scrolls
I have compiled about the world of Avatar. This
scroll contains sacred stories, legends, and facts
that I have gathered so far about the mysterious
Air Nomads—their history, their culture, and the
great tales of their past. I hope that this information
will be as useful and intriguing to you as it is to me.
As a guardian of the Air Nomads' legacy, I ask
that you keep this scroll safe and share it only
with those you trust. Beware, for there are
many who wish to expose its secrets. . . .

# Introduction

降去神通

Water.
Earth.
Fire.
Air.

These are the four nations of our world and the four elements that bind it together.

A few select people of each nation possess the ability to manipulate their native element. They call themselves Waterbenders, Earthbenders, Firebenders, and Airbenders.

The most powerful bender in the world is the Avatar, the spirit of the planet incarnate. Master of all four elements, he maintains world order and keeps the planet balanced and peaceful.

The four nations lived together in harmony until the death of the last Avatar, Avatar Roku. Seizing the opportunity before the next Avatar—an

Airbender—could be found and trained, Fire Lord Sozin led the Fire Nation on a global campaign to wipe out the three other nations.

Only the next Avatar can stop the Fire Nation from conquering the planet, but most people believe he had disappeared during the war on the Air Nomads.

One hundred years after Avatar Roku's death, two teenage siblings have made a discovery that will forever change the destiny of the world: They have found a twelve-year-old boy frozen in an iceberg. His name is Aang, and he is the last Airbender known to be alive. He is also the world's last hope for peace and harmony.

He is . . . the Avatar.

This first legend was passed down from the young Waterbender Katara, who recounts a tale of dashed hopes and enduring faith.

# The Southern Air Temple
## LEGEND 1

My name is Katara and my friend Aang is the Avatar. It's his job to save the world, and it's my job— and my brother's, too—to help him. Of course, I don't know *how* to do that, so I'm hoping it's something I can learn along the way.

My brother, Sokka, and I are members of the **Southern Water Tribe**. We found Aang frozen in an iceberg at the South Pole where we lived. Can you believe that? A frozen boy!

When the Fire Nation launched their war more than one hundred years ago, the first people they attacked were the Air Nomads. No one had seen an Airbender since then.

Aang was an Air Nomad and the only one I'd ever met. I thought he was the last Airbender on the planet, but I didn't want to tell him that right away. You don't just wake up someone from a block of ice and tell him everyone he ever knew is gone.

Aang had been raised at the Southern, Jongmu Air Temple. Now he wanted to see what had happened to it and the other Airbenders he had known. We began our journey to the temple like we usually do, riding through the air on Aang's flying bison, Appa. I have no idea how we'd get around without Appa!

Eventually, the temple appeared on the snow-covered mountain ahead of us. One hundred years ago, when Aang lived here, it must have been beautiful.

Now it just looked forgotten. The stone walls were covered in thick vines and overgrown plants. I didn't think anyone had been there for a long time.

"Aang, I just want you to be prepared for what you might find here," I said. "The Fire Nation is ruthless. They killed my mother. They could have done the same to your people." I didn't want Aang to get his hopes up.

"Relax, Katara," said Aang. "Just because no one has seen an Airbender doesn't mean that the Fire Nation killed them all. Besides, the only way to get to an Airbender temple is on a flying bison. And I doubt the Fire Nation has one."

Aang was so confident, but I still had a bad feeling about this trip. He hadn't really seen what the Fire Nation could do—what it had been doing for a century. Destruction was the Fire Nation's favorite pastime.

"So, where do I get something to eat around here?" my brother said, obviously unconcerned about anything else.

"Sokka, you're lucky enough to be one of the first outsiders to ever visit an Airbender temple, and all you can think about is *food*?" I scolded him.

"I'm just a simple guy with simple needs," he replied. Sometimes Sokka's a little too simple!

"C'mon! We have a whole temple to see!" Aang raced ahead of us and disappeared inside. Food would have to wait! Sokka kicked absently at a cluster of vines, pushing them out of his way.

"Hey, check this out, Katara." Sokka pointed at his feet. There was a tattered Fire Nation flag and two rusty Firebender helmets on the ground.

I knew it! They *had* been here! This was not good.

"Katara, you *have* to tell Aang," said Sokka.

I shook my head. There was no way I was going to tell him. I remembered how I had felt when I lost my mother, and I wanted to protect Aang from that kind of pain.

"Hey, guys!" Aang called from somewhere above us. "Over here! I want you to meet somebody!"

*Somebody?* Who could it be?

Inside the temple, Aang stood in front of a decaying wooden statue of a monk with a bald head and a long mustache. The monk had an arrow tattoo on his head just like Aang's—he was an Airbender too. Aang bowed to the statue.

"Who's that?" Sokka asked.

"Monk Gyatso!" Aang said, rising. "The greatest Airbender in the world. He taught me everything I know. He told me that my questions about being the Avatar would be answered when I was old enough to enter the Airbender sanctuary. I'm ready now."

The sanctuary lay behind two large doors that were splintered and worn with age. Gnarled vines strangled the hinges and covered the doors' ornate, horn-shaped carvings. I don't think anyone had opened the doors in a long time. I hated to imagine what Aang was going to find inside.

"No one could have survived in this sanctuary for a hundred years," I said.

"It's not impossible," Aang replied. "I survived in the iceberg for that long."

I couldn't argue with that. Aang wasn't the only one to survive that long either. Appa had survived with him. If a twelve-year-old Airbender and a flying bison could still be alive, who was I to disagree?

"Whoever's in here might help me figure out this Avatar thing," Aang added. "They could tell me what I'm supposed to do and how I'm supposed to do it."

Sokka tried the doors, but they wouldn't budge. "I don't suppose you have a key?"

Aang laughed. "The key is Airbending." He thrust his hands forward and steadied his feet on the ground, bending his knees slightly. Wind swirled around his arms as he took a deep breath. Air surged into the two horn-shaped carvings on the door. Three clicks sounded from the turning locks and the doors creaked open.

"Hello? Is anyone home?" Aang's voice echoed in the sanctuary.

It was spooky. A chill shivered through my body. In front of us were hundreds of large, wooden statues.

They encircled the room on multiple levels, floor to ceiling.

"Aang, who are all these people?" I asked.

"I'm not sure, but I feel like I know them somehow." Aang pointed to the statue in front of him. "Look, this one's an Airbender, just like me."

The one in front of me was a Waterbender. "They're lined up in a pattern: Air, Water, Earth, Fire."

"That's the Avatar cycle," Aang pointed out.

"They're Avatars!" I realized. "Aang, these people are your past lives."

Aang was awestruck. His eyes scanned the countless statues. "So many . . ."

"Past lives?" Sokka looked at me skeptically. "Oh please, Katara. Do you really believe in that stuff?"

I did believe it because it's true. "When the Avatar dies, he's reincarnated into the next nation in the cycle." Looking around the room, I could see there had been a lot of Avatars before Aang.

Aang examined a statue of a bearded Firebender with long, flowing hair. A glimmer of white light passed over the statue's eyes.

"Aang, who is that?" I asked.

"That's Avatar Roku, the Avatar before me."

"You were a Firebender in your past life?" Sokka asked. "No wonder I didn't trust you when we met."

A long shadow fell across the floor. It looked like a Firebender with a spiked helmet. They must still be here!

"Firebender!" Sokka whispered. He pulled us behind one of the statues as the shadow moved closer. Sokka whipped out his boomerang, ready to attack. The shadow moved closer and was nearly upon us. My heart thumped loudly in my chest. Could we really fight a Firebender on our own?

Sokka leaped out, ready to fight . . . a lemur! What a relief!

The startled lemur jumped into the air and flew out of the sanctuary window.

"Bet you didn't know they could fly!" Aang said as he snapped open his wooden staff and converted it into glider form. He chased the lemur out of the sanctuary with Sokka racing close behind him. I wanted to join in the fun, but I had a lot of things on my mind. I stared into Avatar Roku's blank eyes in silence, thinking about what

Aang had told us. What had Monk Gyatso meant when he told Aang about the sanctuary? I knew the key lay in the Avatar statues. A cold wind blew through the sanctuary doors and I shivered again. I looked around the sanctuary—it was filled with a powerful white light! The eyes of all the Avatar statues were glowing! I could tell that something powerful was happening to the Avatar spirit. I raced from the sanctuary and into the temple courtyard, looking for Aang.

An icy wind caught me by surprise. Aang had created a windstorm! His feet were braced on the ground, spread wide, and his eyes and tattoos glowed like the statues inside. I'd never seen Aang like this before. His arms swirled around him, gathering the air. A huge blast of wind shot from his hands and knocked Sokka backward to the ground!

"Aang!" Sokka's voice trailed off into the wind. "Come on, snap out of it!"

I fought my way through the freezing wind, dodging flying tree branches and broken vines. "Sokka! What happened?"

Sokka crawled to me. "Aang found out the Firebenders were here, and that they killed Gyatso," he yelled. "Then he just started freaking out!"

"It's his Avatar spirit—the shock must have triggered

it!" I yelled. The spirits of the previous Avatars had joined together to give Aang all this power. "I'm going to try to calm him down!"

A tree branch whipped past Sokka's head. "Well, do it before he blows us off the mountain!"

Aang didn't have the full abilities of an Avatar, but he was already pretty powerful—powerful enough to hurt us if I wasn't careful.

I struggled to walk through the strong winds toward Aang. Even though the currents blew me off balance, I knew I had to talk to him. "Aang! I know how hard it is to lose the people you love. . . ." I hoped my voice was strong enough to pierce the wind and reach him. "Monk Gyatso and the other Airbenders may be gone, but you still have a family." We had only known each other a short time, but we shared a strong bond. I hoped Aang felt the same way.

The winds died down. Aang could hear me and I moved closer to him. "Sokka and I, we're your family now."

"Yeah, and we're not going to let anything happen to you," Sokka added. "Promise."

The winds ceased. Swirls of debris fell to the ground around us. I ran to Aang. The glow from his eyes and tattoos faded away and he slumped into my arms, exhausted.

"I'm . . . I'm sorry," Aang said. His voice was hoarse.

"It's okay," I said. "It wasn't your fault."

"If Firebenders found this Air temple, that means they found the other ones, too. I really am the last Airbender." I had never seen Aang so sad or heard his voice so soft before. All of his usual liveliness was gone.

We visited the temple sanctuary one last time. Aang stood in front of the statue of Avatar Roku, waiting for some sign, some clue about his future.

"Any luck?" I was hoping that something would happen.

"Not a peep," Aang replied. "How is Roku supposed to help me if he won't talk to me?"

"Maybe you have to find a way to talk to him," I suggested. I truly believed there might be some way for Aang to communicate with his past lives. We just had to figure it out.

The lemur scampered into the sanctuary with an armful of food and dropped it at Sokka's feet.

"Looks like you made a new friend," Aang said, smiling.

"Can't talk. Must eat." Sokka began to eat hungrily.

The lemur climbed onto Aang and sat on his shoulder.

"Hey, little guy. You, me, and Appa. We're all that's left of this place. We have to stick together. Katara, Sokka, say hello to the newest member of our family: Momo."

I reached out and petted Momo. "We'd better go," I suggested. "We've got a lot of work to do." Now there were five of us: myself, my brother, the Avatar, a flying bison, and a lemur.

Together, we could do a lot.

*Below are the basic details I have managed to find about Air Nomad life, as well as a description of the Avatar Cycle.*

# Air Nomads

The Air Nomads are the most mysterious of all the benders because they disappeared one hundred years ago. They were a peaceful race that was wiped out by the Fire Nation. The Air Nomads lived in huge temples and traveled the world on flying bison. They were the most spiritual of all the cultures and lived in harmony with nature. They also were fun-loving and had a strong sense of humor. Aang is the only known living Air Nomad.

## AIR NOMAD INSIGNIA

The Air Nomad insignia is a stylized swirling orb. Inside the orb, curved lines depict the wind.

## AIR NOMAD FLAG

The Air Nomad flag is a banner held between two wooden poles. The center of the banner is emblazoned with the Air Nomad insignia.

# PHILOSOPHY OF THE AIR NOMADS

As might be expected from people who harness the power of air, the Air Nomads were a peaceful society. Honest and forthright, they preferred to use their powers strictly for defensive purposes.

## SEASON

Autumn is the season of the Airbender. More Air Nomad children were born in this season than any other. Unlike children of the other nations, all Air Nomads were born with bending abilities.

## SHELTER

Air Nomad temples sit atop high mountain peaks, above the clouds. They were carved from stone, with huge spires rising into the sky. The only way to get to the Air temples is on a flying bison.

# ANIMALS OF THE AIR NOMADS

APPA

## FLYING BISON

Flying bison were ancient creatures from which the Airbenders originally learned Airbending. Airbenders' arrow tattoos were adapted from the markings on the bison. The bison were the only nonhuman Airbenders, and they used their wide tails to steer through air currents.

## APPA

Appa, a flying bison, is Aang's lifelong companion. Like all Airbenders, Appa is usually peaceful, but he knows how to protect Aang and his friends.

## WINGED LEMURS

The lemurs were the Air Nomad children's favorite pets. Fun, playful, and highly social, lemurs were trained by the Airbenders to perform many useful tasks, including alerting people of danger.

MOMO

## MOMO

Momo is a flying lemur from the Jongmu Air Temple. Momo means "peach" in Japanese.

# Airbending Basics

## PHILOSOPHY AND STYLE

Airbending is a dynamic skill. Benders use air to enhance natural abilities, allowing one person to defend against multiple attackers from different disciplines. Because no special weapon is required, Airbending is well suited to nomadic life.

## ANCIENT MARTIAL ARTS INFLUENCES

Airbending is similar to the Chinese martial art known as Baguazhang. In Baguazhang, movements employ the whole body with smooth coiling and uncoiling actions, utilizing hand techniques, dynamic footwork, and throws. Rapid-fire movements draw energy from the center of the abdomen.

# TECHNIQUES

Airbending is a highly versatile skill. An Airbender can run faster by decreasing his air resistance and jump higher and farther by creating wind gusts to enhance his motion. An Airbender can protect himself during a fall by forming a wind cushion, and he can run up vertical surfaces such as walls and trees by generating a wind current behind him.

For a high-level attack, an Airbender can create an air vortex to suck in an opponent, spin him around, and spit him out.

He can also create an air dome to shield himself and can deflect attacks with wind gusts.

# SIGNATURE TOOL

An Airbender's signature tool is his wooden staff. Although it does not possess any magical properties, it can transform mechanically into a small glider. To propel the glider, Aang controls air currents to sustain its flight over limited distances. Airbenders also use their staffs as weapons to enhance the amount and power of their attacks and defenses.

# Games

## AIRBALL

Airball was a fast-paced traditional Air Nomad game that relied on an Airbender's speed, balance, and accuracy. Players stood on top of wooden posts and used Airbending skills to pass the ball from one player to another. The goal was to get the ball through the wooden ring on the opponent's side.

## AIR SCOOTER

The Air Scooter was an Airbending move that Aang invented. He swirled a ball of air underneath his body and rode it like a scooter.

## PAI SHO

Pai Sho is an ancient tile game played in all four nations. Combining skill and strategy, many a fortune has been won and lost over a single hand. Aang used to play Pai Sho with Monk Gyatso.

## SKY BISON POLO

Sky Bison Polo was played in the air. Airbenders rode their flying bison and tried to force the ball into an opponent's goal.

The next tale is attributed to the Last Airbender, Aang, who reveals the secret of his legendary disappearance.

# The Storm
## LEGEND 2

My scream woke up Katara and Sokka. I was having the nightmare again.

"Aang! What's going on?" Sokka asked groggily. "Are we under attack?"

"It's nothing," I said. "Just a bad dream. Go back to bed." I hated to think I was keeping my friends awake.

"Don't have to tell me twice." Sokka rolled over and quickly started to snore again. Nothing interferes with his sleep.

My name is Aang, but most people know me only as the Avatar. There's only one thing wrong with that: I don't really know how to be the Avatar yet. The previous

Avatar, Roku, passed away more than one hundred years ago, and he didn't leave behind any instructions. I wish he had!

Katara placed her hand on my shoulder. "You seem to be having a lot of nightmares lately, Aang. You want to tell me about it?"

"Thanks, Katara. I think I just need some rest." I owed Katara and Sokka my life, but I still couldn't tell her what was wrong.

The next morning, we found a busy marketplace by the ocean. Boats lined the long wooden pier, bobbing gently on the calm water. Vendors were selling fish, meat, and fresh vegetables. *Mmmm, vegetables.* My stomach ached for something tasty. I couldn't remember the last real meal we'd eaten.

"What can we get, Katara?" Sokka hungrily eyed the trays of fresh food. He wanted to eat as much as I did.

"Nothing. We're out of money," Katara said.

Uh-oh.

"Great! Now what are we supposed to do?" Sokka whined.

"You could get a job, smart guy," Katara replied. Even though those two bicker a lot, I know they really love each other.

An old fisherman brushed by us, followed by his wife. She grabbed his arm. "Please, don't take the boat out today! There's going to be a big storm!"

"You're crazy!" the fisherman said. "Look at the sky. There's no storm coming!"

The fisherman was right. The sky looked pretty clear to me.

The woman folded her arms. "Find someone else to haul that fish, 'cause I ain't comin'!"

"I'll find a new fish hauler and pay 'em double what you get," the fisherman bragged. "How do you like that?"

Sokka stepped forward. "I'll go!"

I couldn't believe it! Sokka didn't know how to fish and we had to keep moving.

"You're hired," the fisherman snapped, smiling back at his wife.

Sokka saw the look in Katara's eyes. "What? You told me to get a job." He jumped aboard the ship and helped the fisherman load his equipment.

A cool breeze of air made me shiver, and the sky quickly darkened. "Sokka, maybe this isn't such a good idea," I said. The water was choppy now, and I was uncomfortably reminded of something that had happened to me more than a hundred years ago. I was worried about Sokka's safety.

But Sokka was stubborn. "We need money. I can't back out just because of some bad weather." He grabbed a box of tools and headed below deck. His mind was made up.

The fisherman's wife stood on the dock, yelling at her husband. "The boy with the tattoos has some sense! You should listen to him."

The fisherman turned and looked closely at my forehead. I don't think I'll ever get used to being stared at by strangers—although sometimes it is kind of flattering. "Airbender tattoos . . . well, I'll be a hog monkey's uncle. You're the Avatar!"

"That's right!" Katara said proudly.

"Well, don't be so smiley about it!" he snapped. "The Avatar disappeared for a hundred years!" He pointed an accusing finger at me. "You turned your back on the world."

"Don't yell at him!" Katara said. "Aang would never turn his back on anyone."

"Oh, he wouldn't? Then I guess I must have imagined the last century of war and suffering."

"Aang is the bravest person I know," Katara said. "He's done nothing but help people and save lives since I met him. It's not his fault that he disappeared for all those years. Right, Aang?"

Katara turned to me, waiting for my answer. I knew what she wanted to hear, but I couldn't say it. I didn't want to admit the truth, but I couldn't lie to Katara either. So I ran away from Katara and the fisherman and back through the market. I heard the fisherman's words in my head, stinging me.

Katara found me in a seaside cave several minutes later. "Are you okay?"

"I'm sorry I ran, Katara," I said. "The fisherman was right. I let everyone down. It's all my fault."

"This is about your nightmare, isn't it?" Sometimes Katara can be so perceptive. She knelt down and put a hand on my shoulder.

I took a deep breath. It was time to tell her the truth. "Monk Gyatso told me I was the Avatar when I was twelve. He was supposed to wait until I was sixteen, but the monks were worried that Fire Lord Sozin was going to start the war before then. They needed time to train me."

"Weren't you excited about being the Avatar?"

"I was at first. Who wouldn't be? But then everything changed. I wasn't just Aang anymore. My friends didn't want to play with me because they thought I had an unfair advantage. I had to train every day, all day long, and the only person I could really talk to was Monk Gyatso. He was the only one who treated me like a normal kid."

I looked out of the cave and saw clouds sweeping across the sky, cutting off the sun. Thunder boomed around us as lightning crackled in the distance. It began to rain, and I thought of Sokka out there on the open sea. I hoped he was okay.

"The other monks thought I had too much fun with Monk Gyatso. I heard them making plans to send me to the Eastern Air Temple to complete my training."

Katara reached out to comfort me, but I pulled away. "I couldn't let them take everything from me! So Appa and I ran away. But somewhere over the ocean we were caught in a storm just like this one. Next thing I knew, you found me in the iceberg. A hundred years had passed.

"After I left, the Fire Nation attacked our temple. My people needed me and I wasn't there to help! The fisherman was right: I am the Avatar. I'm supposed to help people, but I ran away when the world needed me most." I hung my head, my cheeks burning with shame.

"You're being too hard on yourself." Katara wrapped her arm around my shoulder. "I think it was meant to be. If you hadn't run away, you would have been killed with the other Airbenders. The world needs you now, and you're here now."

"Help!" The fisherman's wife rushed through the rain. "My husband's boat is still out there!"

Katara and I looked out at the sea. Rain poured from black clouds while gigantic waves surged toward the shore, driven by the violent winds.

I made up my mind. "We'll find them."

"Where are they?" Katara yelled.

I couldn't see the fishing boat anywhere. We were flying miles from shore through the storm. Pummeling rain stung my skin and lightning crackled through the sky. Suddenly a monstrous wave loomed over us.

I pulled on Appa's reins. "Yip-yip!" He banked upward, trying to fly over the wave. I can always count on Appa to come through for me. But the wave kept growing higher and higher. Katara and I ducked our heads as Appa broke through the crest.

We burst through the other side and rose above the turbulent ocean. Salt water stung my eyes. Lightning flashed twice ahead of us. I saw a small object floating in the distance. We had found Sokka and the fisherman, and just in time.

The tiny fishing boat was no match for the fierce sea. Waves crashed over the deck, pounding it like a hammer. I was afraid it was going to sink before we could reach them.

Sokka and the fisherman clung desperately to a pile of rope on deck. I guided Appa toward the boat and jumped aboard. The boat rocked so much, I almost fell into the ocean.

Lightning struck the mast, and the heavy wooden pole started to fall toward us. I bent a rush of air at the mast and it crashed onto the deck next to us.

"Hold on!" I yelled. Sokka and the fisherman caught the end of the rope I threw to them. As I jumped into Appa's saddle, I snapped the rope like a whip, yanking them aboard.

34

In my rush to rescue Sokka and the fisherman, I'd ignored the ocean. Once again, the shadow of an immense wave fell over us. This time we couldn't avoid it.

The wave crested and crashed against Appa. We were thrown into the surging ocean. I almost froze at the shock of the cold water!

I thought about the storm from my past—the storm in my nightmares that had frozen me for a hundred years. I wasn't going to let anyone down this time. I wasn't going to run away. Gathering my last strength, I fought the current, pushing at the water to create an air bubble around me.

I made a wider arc with my arms, enlarging the bubble so that it encircled all of us. We could breathe now. We climbed aboard Appa while the ocean pounded against our bubble.

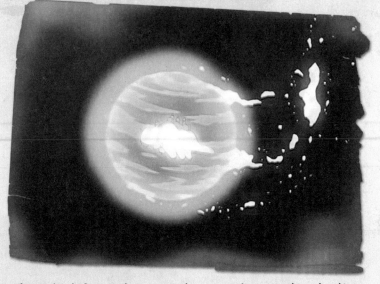

I guided Appa through the swirling water to the eye of the storm, where the sea was calm. We emerged from the water and flew above the clouds into the clear blue sky.

"All right!" Sokka yelled.

I looked below us and almost gasped. We had made it! We were safe!

As Appa swooped through the air, we narrowly avoided a small Fire Nation ship—and at the helm was Prince Zuko, who had been trying to capture me for weeks! For a moment I was afraid he might decide to pursue us. But I could tell from the look in his eyes that he knew his men needed him to lead them through the storm. We looked at each other for a split second, and in that one moment, I felt that we were almost kindred spirits.

A few minutes later we were back on land and the storm was over. The fisherman's wife rushed toward us and hugged her husband.

I turned to Katara. "You were right. I'm done dwelling on the past. I can't make guesses about how things would have turned out if I hadn't run away," I said. "I'm here now and I have a job to do."

I was the Avatar and I knew I could do good things for people.

The fisherman held out his hand. "If you weren't here now, Avatar, then I guess I wouldn't be either. Thank you for saving my life."

"I don't think you're going to have those nightmares anymore," Katara said to me.

I didn't think so either. My new life had begun.

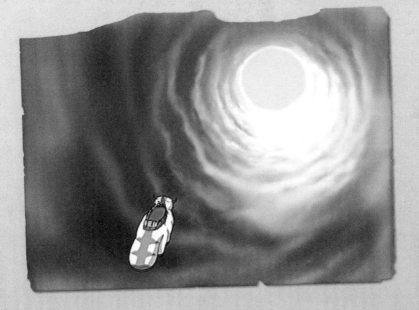

## AIR NOMAD MONKS

The Air Nomads were led by an order of monks. The monks taught the future generations of Airbenders. They were also responsible for training the new Avatar each time the cycle returned to Air. Many of the monks, like Monk Gyatso, were also excellent bakers! They made fruit pies, delicious dumplings, and many kinds of inventive desserts.

38

MONK GYATSO

## LOCATION

The monks lived in four temples, all at high altitudes. There are temples located at each compass point—north, south, east, and west. Air Nomads not linked to a temple had no permanent home and roamed the world individually or in groups.

## MEDITATION

Meditation was an important part of Airbenders' daily routines. It helped them focus their energy and understand the power of the air.

# Becoming the Avatar

## LEVELS OF AIRBENDING

One must master Airbending to earn the arrow tattoos. To do this, an Airbender must invent a new move and pass the thirty-six levels of Airbending. Though Aang had only reached the thirty-fifth level before he left the Jongmu Temple, his invention of the Air Scooter earned him his tattoos early.

## IDENTIFYING THE AVATAR

At an early age, Aang was able to pick out the Avatar relics, toys that had belonged to the previous Air Nomad Avatars. This convinced the monks that he was the reincarnated spirit of the Avatar.

# TRAINING THE AVATAR

According to Airbender custom, monks tell the Avatar of his status on his sixteenth birthday. Only then can his training officially begin. Aang was told early, at age twelve, because the monks were afraid that Fire Lord Sozin was preparing for war and they needed the Avatar's help.

# THE AVATAR CYCLE

The Avatar is the human incarnation of the spirit of the planet. When an Avatar dies, his spirit is reincarnated into the next nation in the Avatar Cycle: Water, Earth, Fire, Air. For example, Avatar Roku was a Firebender. When he died, his spirit passed to Aang, an Airbender. When Aang dies, his spirit will pass to a Waterbender, then to an Earthbender.

Upon the death of an Avatar, bending masters from the next nation begin to look for the Avatar reincarnate.

The Avatar is the only person who can bend all four elements— Water, Earth, Fire, and Air— and his job is to keep the four nations in harmony with one another. The Avatar must master his own bending element before he can train with masters of the remaining elements.

WATER

AIR

## AVATARS BEFORE AANG

Past Avatars like Roku and Kyoshi are honored with statues in the Southern Air Temple and their respective nations. There have been both male and female Avatars throughout history.

# THE AVATAR STATE

When his eyes turn white hot and his tattoos glow and pulse, Aang has entered the Avatar state. The Avatar state is triggered by extreme physical or emotional stress. In this way, the Avatar can send a kind of psychic distress signal to his spirit. All the past Avatars can help Aang in this way, enhancing his strength and power. The Avatar state kept Aang alive in the iceberg for one hundred years.

EARTH

FIRE

# Aang vs. Zuko

Though they are on opposite sides of Fire Lord Sozin's war, Aang and Zuko have many similarities. Both are on their own, but do have father figures. Aang was taken from his parents when they discovered he was the Avatar, but Monk Gyatso took him under his wing. Prince Zuko's father, Fire Lord Ozai, banished him from the Fire Nation for daring to disagree with his policies, but Uncle Iroh keeps an eye on his fiery nephew.

Aang and Zuko also have shameful pasts. They both have to live with the guilt of disappointing the people they cared about the most. Aang is marked by the traditional Airbender tattoos, and Zuko was scarred in a duel with his father. Aang and Zuko have companions on their opposing quests. Zuko and Aang are both benders who are fighting for something: Aang fights to save the world; Zuko fights to save his honor.

Before the war broke out, Aang used to have many Firebender friends, but Zuko has only just met Aang; Aang is interested in Zuko as a person, but Zuko only sees Aang as a means to regain his honor.

This tale was passed down from the young warrior Sokka, who details his role in a battle against the Fire Nation.

# The Northern Air Temple

## LEGEND 3

"Sokka, do you really think we'll find Airbenders?" Katara whispered.

My sister is a total optimist. I tend to see things a *little* more clearly. "Do you want me to be like you, or totally honest?" I replied. Katara and I were on our way to the Northern Air Temple with our friend Aang. A man had told us he'd seen Airbenders there. Supposedly Aang was the last Airbender, but he and Katara were hoping that the rumor was true. I guess that makes both of them total optimists. Appa soared through the clouds as he climbed higher into the sky. Then the temple appeared, shrouded in mist on a high mountaintop.

Its stone spires poked through the clouds and into the sky. It was quite impressive, if you like that kind of thing. But I was more impressed by the people who swooped through the air around it.

"Those guys are flying!" I said, amazed. Katara was right—she would never let me hear the end of this.

"Oh, Aang! They really are Airbenders!" she said.

Aang's smile faded. "No, they're not."

"What do you mean?" I said.

"I can tell by the way they move, they're not Airbending," Aang said sadly.

One of the gliders flew past us in a chairlike contraption. "Hi, I'm Teo!" He waved at us as he passed by. What a show-off.

Aang leaped from the bison and snapped open his staff, catching a rush of air to fly alongside Teo. They swooped and looped under and around us, keeping pace with each other.

"Maybe we'd better find some solid ground before it finds us," I suggested. Katara and I guided Appa down to the temple grounds, where a crowd of excited kids watched Aang and Teo soaring side by side.

Teo swooped higher into the air. He did a series of tumbles that brought him back to eye level with Aang, except that Teo was now upside down! Then Aang flew into a big loop, ending with a series of flips. Teo and Aang were showing off, but it was great to watch.

Aang banked and soared toward the temple and landed next to me.

Teo dropped from the air like a falling feather. His speed and twirling increased until he was a spinning blur. As he approached the temple, he grabbed a banner pole. He swung on it several times and landed right in front of us. The wheels on his glider skidded to a stop.

I noticed then that Teo's legs were wrapped in white cloth. He couldn't walk. That made his flying ability even more impressive.

"Hey, you're a *real* Airbender," Teo said to Aang. "You must be the Avatar! I've heard stories about you."

While Teo and Aang got acquainted, I studied Teo's chair. Its mechanics were amazing! Whoever designed it sure knew a lot about air currents.

Teo saw me examining the glider. "If you think that's good," he said, "wait until you see all the other stuff my dad has invented."

I could hardly wait!

I stood, speechless, inside the hall of the Air Temple—an enormous room filled with whizzing, whirring machines. Large wooden wheels rotated, pulling giant ropes. Steam pipes jutted from the cracked plaster walls. A complex elevator system carried people from one level to the next using steam and pulleys. I had never seen anything like it.

"My dad is the mastermind behind this whole place," said Teo.

"Unbelievable," Aang said.

"Yeah, it's great, isn't it?" Teo smiled with pride.

"No, just unbelievable." Aang turned and walked away.

"Aang used to come here a long time ago," Katara explained to Teo. "I think he's a little shocked it's so . . . different."

"So *better*!" I added. And it was too. Teo's dad was a genius! I couldn't wait to meet him.

Teo smiled and nodded.

"What the doodle?" said Teo's dad, the Mechanist, as he rushed over to us. He looked like an owl, with his shock of brown hair, patchy eyebrows, and a thin red scar around one eye. This was a true man of science.

Too bad Aang didn't see it that way. "This is a sacred temple!" he said. "You can't do this. I was here a long time ago, and I know what it's supposed to be like!" Aang was still getting used to the new world around him, realizing just how much the Fire Nation has changed everything.

Teo's father studied Aang for a few seconds, examining the arrow tattoo on his bald head. I knew he was trying to figure out how a kid could have seen the temple as it used to be. I think sometimes Aang forgets that *normal* people don't get frozen in icebergs for a century at a time like him.

"Dad, he's the Avatar," Teo explained. "He used to come here a hundred years ago."

"Who said you could live here?" Aang demanded.

The Mechanist paced the stone floor. "A few years ago, my people had to flee a flood. I lost my wife, and Teo was badly hurt. We needed a place to rebuild."

"Of course!" I realized. "And it needed to be safe from floods, so you looked high in the mountains."

"That's right!" he said. "I stumbled across this place. Couldn't believe it. Pictures of flying people everywhere! But there was no one here."

He spread his arms out like wings. "Then I came across these flying machines."

"Our gliders," Aang said.

"Yes! They gave me an idea: Build a new life for my son . . . in the air! That way everyone would be on equal ground, so to speak."

Teo took Katara and Aang on a tour of the temple while the Mechanist showed me his workshop. What an operation! He was working on dozens of projects. Charts and scrolls were stuffed into every nook and cranny. The man had plans for machines that no one had thought of before. He showed me a prototype of a hot-air balloon that could carry a hen's egg through the air. I felt privileged to get a glimpse of how this guy's mind worked.

A loud bell rang in the workshop. Alarmed, the Mechanist raced out the door. I followed right behind, hoping he would let me help him fix whatever invention wasn't working. I could learn a lot from this guy.

I caught up to the Mechanist at the entrance to the temple's sanctuary. Aang, Katara, and Teo stood in the doorway, staring. Swords, arrows, spiked metal wheels, pieces of armor, and other weapons I didn't recognize filled the large room. But I *did* recognize the Fire Nation insignia.

"You make weapons for the Fire Nation!" I was stunned.

Teo looked furiously at his father. "Explain this. Now."

The Mechanist looked trapped. He sighed. "A year after we moved here, Fire Nation soldiers found our settlement," he said quietly. "You were too young to remember, Teo. They were going to destroy everything, burn it to the ground. I pleaded with them and they asked what I had to offer." The Mechanist took a deep, sad breath. "I offered my services."

I couldn't believe it. This *genius* was working for the Fire Nation! How could he do such a thing?

"When are they coming back?" Aang asked sharply.

"Soon," the Mechanist said. "Very soon."

"You can't give them more weapons," Aang said. It was not a request. I couldn't agree more, but the Fire Nation doesn't take no for an answer. I knew we would have to fight them.

Katara, Aang, Teo, and I stood on the balcony overlooking the mountains. The Fire Nation soldiers would arrive soon, and while the temple is a natural fortress, I doubted we could defeat them. "This is bad, very bad," I said.

"We can take them, Sokka," Aang said. "We've done it before."

"I don't think you understand, Aang," I explained. "Teo's dad told me the mountain is full of natural gas." I pointed down a deep crevasse. "Just one spark of flame could send this whole place sky high. How can we stop Firebenders from Firebending?"

"We can keep them away from the mountain. We have something they don't." Aang pointed to the sky. "Air power: We control the sky!"

"He's right," Teo agreed. "We can win this." I wasn't so sure.

The Mechanist joined us. "I have something in my workshop that can help." He smiled at me, and I remembered something I had seen downstairs. We did have a chance!

We were ready by the time the Fire Nation soldiers arrived. They marched single file up the steep mountain path, stomping their heavy boots into the packed snow.

Aang and Teo attacked from the air, dropping stink, smoke, fire, and slime bombs from their gliders. The soldiers were pushed back down the mountain. Then Aang shot a current of air at the mountainside, creating an avalanche of snow. The pass was blocked. Score one for our side.

But the soldiers had a way around it. Huge tanks rolled up the cliffs, spitting flames. It was time for me and the Mechanist to join the fight. I couldn't wait!

I tightened the valve on the giant Warballoon. It was just like the prototype I had seen in the workshop, only this model was one hundred feet high and carried something much more effective than eggs: a half dozen slime bombs hung from the side.

Our balloon flew over the temple and the Fire Nation soldiers. They paid us no attention because the balloon was marked with the Fire Nation insignia.

"They think we're on their side," the Mechanist said.

"Then I guess they won't expect this!" I cut one of the ropes. "Bombs away!"

Bull's-eye! The bomb splattered below us, covering the Fire Nation tanks and soldiers in sticky gunk.

They froze in place, unable to move. I carefully cut the other bombs loose as we floated by. Each one found its mark, halting the tanks' advance. We were winning, but more tanks kept coming and we had run out of bombs.

"What are we going to do now?" I asked. The tanks were closing in on the temple. There had to be something we could do. I didn't want to lose this battle.

Down on the ground, I saw Aang twirling his staff, sending blasts of air at the tanks. The gusts flew under the machines and flipped them over, but he couldn't hold them all off.

"We're losing," I yelled. "What else do you have in your workshop?"

"Not in my workshop, Sokka," the Mechanist said. "Down there—the gas in the mountain!" He pointed to a fissure in the rocks below.

Of course! That gave me an idea. I grabbed our balloon's heating unit and ripped it from the floor.

"What are you doing? That's our fuel source!" the Mechanist shouted.

"It's also the only bomb we've got left," I explained.

He smiled. We tossed the flaming fuel container over the side of the balloon and watched it crash into the fissure. Our aim was excellent!

A huge explosion blew the Fire Nation tanks from the mountainside. Their metal shells collapsed into the valley below and were buried in a landslide. The Fire Nation was forced to retreat. Today was our day!

Together, we had used science and invention to defeat the Fire Nation. But we had one more problem. Without its heating unit, our balloon was slowly falling from the sky toward the rocks below.

"Hang on!" Aang leaped from the temple and hit the air. He steered his glider toward our sinking balloon.

I looped a rope around my boomerang. When Aang flew past, I threw the boomerang around his glider. The Mechanist grabbed on to my end of the rope just as the rope tightened and pulled us from the balloon. Aang carried us to safety as our balloon crashed into the trees below.

We all celebrated when we returned to the temple. The Fire Nation had been defeated for now. Teo's people could live in peace, and his father wouldn't have to work for the enemy anymore. The Mechanist would have more time to invent things for his own people.

Aang took one last look around the temple. "I'm really glad you guys live here now," he said to Teo.

"Really?"

Aang picked up a hermit crab that scrambled past his feet. "It's like the hermit crab: Maybe you weren't born here, but you found this empty shell and made it your home. And now you protect each other."

"That means a lot coming from the Avatar," Teo said.

"You were right about air power, Aang," I told him. "As long as we've got the skies, we'll have the Fire Nation on the run!"

# The Legacy

Though the Air Nomads appear to have been wiped from the Earth, elements of their legacy linger. The largest permanent structures they built were the four Air temples. Places for learning, quiet meditation, and the study and practice of Airbending, their grounds featured reflecting pools, grassy fields for outdoor games, gardens, historical murals, statues, and more.

Time has changed their appearance and function. The uninhabited Southern Air Temple is now overgrown with vegetation. The Northern Air Temple is now occupied by a band of refugees from the Earth Kingdom who are remodeling the temple to suit their needs.

# Technology
## POWER SOURCE

Airbenders derived their power from the air. They could channel a light breeze into the force of a tornado and ride air currents like they were flying. Air was the most important natural resource to Airbenders. Without air, they were powerless. With air under their control, they could protect and defend anyone, even against the Fire Nation.

# INDUSTRIES

The Air Nomads were peaceful and environmentally friendly. They tried not to leave a mark on the land, and any industries they created, such as farming and gardening, were powered naturally. They also produced their own food.

# THE MECHANIST'S INVENTIONS

The Mechanist has taken over the Northern Air Temple for his fellow refugees and is remodeling it with his inventions.

The Mechanist is good at lifting people to new heights. Inside the temple they can move quickly between levels by using the compressed-air elevator. Outside they can soar through the air in their custom-built gliders.

Even his smallest inventions were designed to be useful. Notched candles filled with spark powder are clocks; they spark the time every hour. The Mechanist's jointed wooden fingers replaced the ones he lost while making his finger-safe knife sharpener. Fireflies in paper lanterns are bright but, unlike torches, don't use fire—very important in a mountain containing natural gas!

Larger inventions are just as practical, although they can sometimes be dangerous: The enormous, steam-powered telescope gave the Mechanist his trademark circular scar!

Of all of the Mechanist's creations, the Warballoon may be the greatest. Using hot air, it is able to fly long distances while carrying a heavy load of large slime bombs.

# Epilogue

## THE POWER OF THE AIR

should never be underestimated, especially when it's in the hands of the last Airbender. From Jongmu to the Northern Air Temple, Aang had searched for his people, only to realize that he truly was the last of his kind. The defeat of the Fire Nation at the Northern Air Temple was only one victory in a larger war. The Fire Nation will continue its hunt for the Avatar and its quest for world domination, strengthened by the return of Sozin's Comet, which is expected by the end of the summer. It is then that Fire Lord Ozai will use the comet's immense power to finish the war once and for all.

As I conclude and seal this scroll, Aang has already played a larger role in an epic battle, helping the Northern Water Tribe to defeat Admiral Zhao's navy at the North Pole. The Fire Nation is regrouping, and Aang is on his way to mastering the three remaining elements: water, earth, and fire. This is all I know so far. Please do not show this scroll to anyone whose trustworthiness you doubt. The fate of the world is in your hands!

降去神通